GW01550993

For Saskia
M.W.

First published 1999 by Walker Books Ltd
87 Vauxhall Walk, London SE11 5HJ

This edition published 2005

2 4 6 8 10 9 7 5 3 1

Text © 1999 Martin Waddell
Illustrations © 1999, 2005 Barbara Firth

The right of Martin Waddell and Barbara Firth to be
identified as author and illustrator respectively of this work
has been asserted by them in accordance with the
Copyright, Designs and Patents Act 1988

This book has been typeset in Monotype Columbus

Printed in China

All rights reserved

British Library Cataloguing in Publication Data:
a catalogue record for this book
is available from the British Library

ISBN 1-84428-057-8 (hb)
ISBN 1-84428-493-X (pb)

www.walkerbooks.co.uk

WALKER BOOKS
AND SUBSIDIARIES
LONDON • BOSTON • SYDNEY • AUCKLAND

Well Done,
Little Bear

Martin Waddell

illustrated by **Barbara Firth**

Once there were two bears,

Big Bear and Little Bear.

Big Bear is the big bear

and Little Bear is the little bear.

One day, Little Bear wanted

to go exploring.

Little Bear led the way.

Little Bear found Bear Rock.

"Look at me!" Little Bear said.

"Where are you, Little Bear?" asked Big Bear.

"I'm exploring Bear Rock,"

Little Bear said. "Watch me climb."

"Well done, Little Bear,"

said Big Bear.

"I need you now, Big Bear,"

Little Bear shouted. "I'm jumping."

"I'm here, Little Bear," said Big Bear.

Little Bear jumped off Bear Rock

into the arms of Big Bear.

"I'm off exploring again!"

Little Bear said and he ran

on in front of Big Bear.

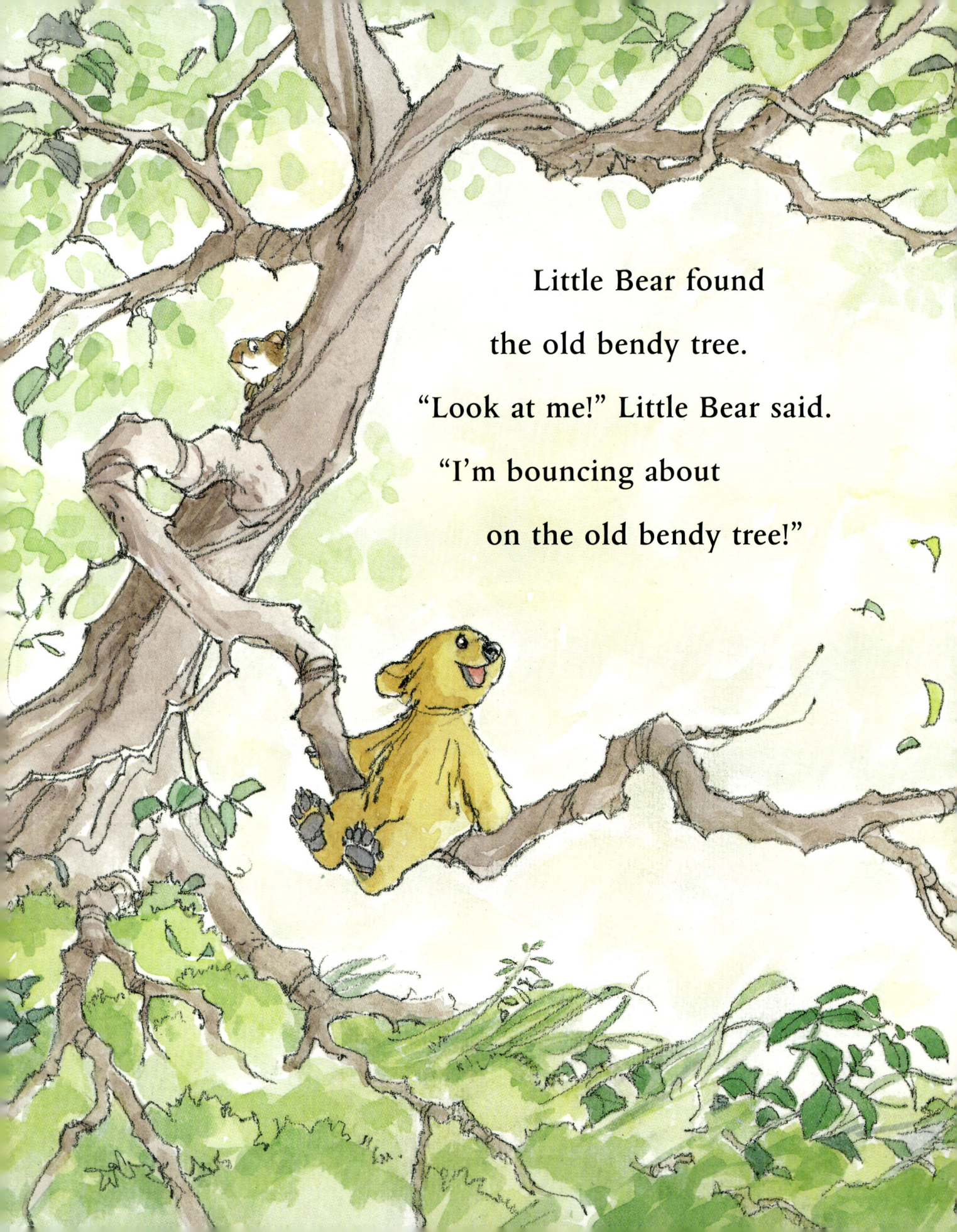

Little Bear found

the old bendy tree.

"Look at me!" Little Bear said.

"I'm bouncing about

on the old bendy tree!"

Little Bear bounced on the branch.

"Watch me bounce higher,

Big Bear!" Little Bear said.

"Well done, Little Bear," said Big Bear.

"Are you ready, Big Bear?"

Little Bear called to Big Bear.

Little Bear bounced

higher and higher

and he bounced

off the branch ...

right into the arms of Big Bear.

"You caught me again!" Little Bear said.

"Well done, Little Bear," said Big Bear.

"I'm going exploring some more!"

Little Bear said.

Little Bear found the stream, just by the dark bit.

"I'm going over the stream," Little Bear said.

"Look at me, Big Bear. Look at me crossing

the stream by myself."

"Well done, Little Bear,"

said Big Bear.

Little Bear hopped from one stone to another.

"I'm the best hopper there is!" Little Bear said.

Little Bear hopped again,

and again.

"Take care, Little Bear," said Big Bear.

"I am taking care," Little Bear said.

"Little Bear…!"

called Big Bear…

"Help me, Big Bear,"

Little Bear cried.

Big Bear waded in, and he pulled

Little Bear out of the water.

"Don't cry, Little Bear," Big Bear said.

"We'll soon have you dry."

He hugged Little Bear.

"Let's go exploring some more,

   Little Bear," said Big Bear.

"Exploring where?" Little Bear asked.

"On the far side of the stream," said Big Bear.

"Take care, Big Bear, you might fall

   in like me," Little Bear said.

"Not if you show me the stone

   where you slipped," said Big Bear.

   "It was this stone," Little Bear said.

   "Well done, Little Bear!"

      said Big Bear.

Big Bear and Little Bear explored
their way home through the woods,
all the way back to the Bear Cave.

Big Bear and Little Bear settled down

cosy and warm in the Bear Chair.

"Were you scared, Little Bear?" asked Big Bear.

"Were you scared when you fell in the water?"

"I knew you'd be there," Little Bear said.

"That's right, Little Bear," said Big Bear.

"I'll be there when

you need me …

always."